# Caught in the Act

The story Jessica had handed in was on top! Keeping her eyes on Mrs. Becker, she reached out to take the paper.

"Jessica?" Mrs. Becker said, turning around. "Do you need something?"

Jessica's face was bright pink. "I um . . . I wanted to make a correction on my story. I just want to make a teensy change."

Mrs. Becker frowned. "I have already read it, Jessica. It's very good." She paused. "So is Elizabeth's."

Jessica thought she would cry. "I don't want you to count that story," she said. "I didn't . . . I didn't . . ." Jessica gulped.

Bantam Skylark Books in the
  SWEET VALLEY KIDS series
Ask your bookseller for the
  books you have missed

SWEET VALLEY KIDS

# JESSICA'S BIG MISTAKE

Created by
Francine Pascal

Written by
Molly Mia Stewart

Illustrated by
Ying-Hwa Hu

A BANTAM SKYLARK BOOK®
NEW YORK • TORONTO • LONDON • SYDNEY • AUCKLAND

RL 2, 005-008

JESSICA'S BIG MISTAKE
*A Bantam Skylark Book / May 1990*

*Sweet Valley High® and Sweet Valley Kids are trademarks of
Francine Pascal*

*Conceived by Francine Pascal*

*Produced by Daniel Weiss Associates, Inc.
33 West 17th Street
New York, NY 10011*

*Cover art by Susan Tang*

*Skylark Books is a registered trademark of Bantam Books, a division of
Bantam Doubleday Dell Publishing Group, Inc.*

ISBN 0-553-15799-X

*Published simultaneously in the United States and Canada*

*Bantam Books are published by Bantam Books, a division of Bantam Double-
day Dell Publishing Group, Inc. Its trademark, consisting of the words
"Bantam Books" and the portrayal of a rooster, is Registered in U.S. Patent
and Trademark Office and in other countries. Marca Registrada. Bantam
Books, 666 Fifth Avenue, New York, New York 10103.*

*To William Benjamin Rubin*

# CHAPTER 1

# A Surprise Visitor

Elizabeth Wakefield was frowning down at her book. "As—astro—," she sounded out loud. It was a difficult word.

Mrs. Becker, her teacher, nodded. "You can do it."

"Astronomer?" Elizabeth asked, looking up.

Mrs. Becker smiled. "Good. Who knows what an astronomer is?" she asked the class.

No one said anything. Elizabeth wished she knew. She looked over at her identical twin sister, Jessica, who was sitting next to her.

"Do you know?" Elizabeth whispered.

Jessica looked surprised. "What page are we on?" she asked. She was writing a note instead of reading along.

Jessica never really listened in class. She believed school was made for whispering with friends and for playing during recess. Elizabeth was just the opposite. She liked all her subjects and always did her homework on time. Her favorite class was reading. Jessica joked that *her* favorite class was lunch.

People didn't always realize that identical twins could be so different. Even some of the other kids in Mrs. Becker's second-grade class thought Jessica and Elizabeth were the same inside and out.

The twins did look the same on the outside. In fact, they looked like two peas in a pod. Both had long blond hair with bangs, and large blue-green eyes. Usually they picked the same outfits, although Jessica picked hers in pink and Elizabeth chose blue or green. Some of their clothes were the same color, though, and when they dressed exactly alike, no one could tell them apart!

Elizabeth thought it was fun to confuse people sometimes. She loved everything about being a twin. She liked sharing a bedroom and sharing cookies, and she and Jessica could often tell what the other was thinking. Being identical twins meant being best friends.

"Does anyone know what an astronomer is?" Mrs. Becker asked again.

Andy Franklin raised his hand. "It's a person who learns about the stars," he said.

Charlie Cashman threw a spitball at Andy. It hit him on the side of the head.

"That's enough, Charlie," Mrs. Becker said. "All right, Elizabeth. Keep reading to the end of the paragraph."

Elizabeth read out loud in a clear voice. The book was a new story by Angela Daley, her favorite author. She already knew she wanted to read it again later, by herself.

"Now, I have an announcement I think you're all going to like," Mrs. Becker said cheerfully.

Kids started whispering and looking at one another. Elizabeth glanced at Jessica and grinned. Her sister looked excited.

"A special visitor is coming to our class next week," Mrs. Becker continued. She smiled. "Angela Daley will spend the morning with us."

Elizabeth gasped. "Wow!"

"I knew it!" Lila Fowler whispered. She sat

on the other side of Jessica. "I told you I saw a letter from her on Mrs. Becker's desk. I told you!"

Jessica's eyes widened. "A real author? I bet she's really rich and famous."

"Oh! Mrs. Becker?" Caroline Pearce was waving her hand in the air. "Can she autograph my book? I have *Hedgehog Holiday.*"

Elizabeth gasped again. She had every one of Angela Daley's books. Maybe the author would sign them all. Elizabeth could just imagine what the autograph would look like: "To my biggest fan, Elizabeth, from Angela Daley."

"Yes, she will autograph books after she tells us what it's like to be a writer," Mrs. Becker explained. "And I'll pick one person to help her with the autographing."

"Oh!" Caroline almost jumped out of her chair to raise her hand. "I'll help. Can I?"

Mrs. Becker chuckled. "Anyone who wants to be chosen should do something special to welcome Mrs. Daley to our class. You could write a book report, or make a poster, anything you like. But it should be something about books."

Elizabeth was so excited that she didn't even care about being picked. Just meeting Angela Daley would be enough. She couldn't wait.

# CHAPTER 2

# Jessica's Plan

After school, Elizabeth went over to Amy Sutton's house, while Jessica and Lila went to the park. Mrs. Wakefield sat on a bench with some other parents.

"Do you want to go on the seesaw?" Jessica asked Lila. She tipped one of the seesaws up so one end bumped on the ground.

"OK," Lila said. Jessica ran to the other end and waited for Lila to push off before getting on. Then she pushed up into the air.

On the next seesaw, Caroline Pearce and

Sandy Ferris were waving their arms up and down like birds.

"What do you think Mrs. Daley will be like?" Lila wondered out loud. "I bet she's very glamorous."

Lila was always using words like "glamorous" and "celebrity." The Fowler family was very rich, and Lila's father knew a lot of famous people. Jessica made a face at her.

"Do you think she'll wear a diamond necklace and gold bracelets?" Jessica asked.

Lila nodded in a know-it-all way. "Oh, sure. Famous people always wear a lot of jewelry. And she probably has a limousine."

"Is that one of those long cars with windows you can't see into?" Sandy asked. Her eyes were wide and curious.

Lila nodded again. "Yes," she said in a

stuck-up voice. "I've been in them lots of times."

"I guess the person Mrs. Becker picks will have an important job," Jessica said dreamily. She was sure it would be fun to be in front of the class with a famous author. Jessica loved being in the spotlight. Only she didn't know what to do to get picked.

"I'm going to give Angela Daley something very special," Caroline said.

Lila raised her eyebrows. "*I'm* going to get her the best welcome present," she said.

Jessica's stomach did a flip-flop. Lila's father was rich enough to buy anything! "It's not supposed to be something you buy," she reminded her friend. "It's supposed to be something you do, like writing a book report."

"It doesn't have to be," Lila said, shaking her head. "I say it can be anything."

"You don't get to decide!" Caroline shouted. "Mrs. Becker does! I'm telling her what you said."

Lila stuck her tongue out at Caroline and then pretended she wasn't there.

Jessica was worried that Lila would be picked just for getting an expensive present. "She's right," she said, even though she didn't like to agree with Caroline. "Besides, I know the perfect plan for getting picked, *so there*, Lila."

Lila pouted and stopped seesawing. "What is it?"

"I'm not telling," Jessica said mysteriously.

Jessica really didn't have a plan yet. But she didn't want Lila to know that.

"I already know what I'm giving her," Caroline said. "I'm giving her a special pen to autograph books with. She'll like that."

Lila made a horrible face. "Yuck! That pen you chew on in class?" She looked at Jessica and they both giggled. "She'll hate it!"

"No!" Caroline said. "A nice new one." Her face got red and she didn't say anything more.

Maybe Jessica didn't know how to get picked. But she was sure she could think of a better idea than Caroline's.

She just had to think of a better idea than Lila's. Then she would get to be a star for a day.

# CHAPTER 3

## Elizabeth's Idea

Elizabeth lay on her stomach on Amy's bed. Spread all around were copies of Angela Daley's books.

"You have all the ones I have," Elizabeth said after she counted them all. "But I also have *Beetle Birthday* and *Kangaroo Campers,* too.

Amy was trying to get a knot out of her hair. "I'm getting those two on my birthday," she answered. "Then I'll have all of her books."

"Which is your favorite?" Elizabeth asked.

She picked up *Hedgehog Holiday* and flipped through the pages.

Amy looked up. "That one. I love it when all the hedgehogs in the school get on the bus with their suitcases and their beach balls and sunglasses and stuff."

Giggling, Elizabeth turned to a picture of the plump hedgehogs waiting in line to get onto the bus.

"You know what?" she said. "This one looks like Andy Franklin." She held out the book and pointed to a little hedgehog with glasses.

Amy's eyes crinkled at the corners. "You're right! And those two that are holding hands look like you and Jessica. See? They're wearing the same outfits."

Elizabeth looked at the pictures again.

14

There were two hedgehogs that looked like twins. She smiled and put the book down.

"Wouldn't it be great to be a writer like Angela Daley?" she sighed. "It must be the best thing in the whole world."

Amy began piling up her books. "It sure would be fun."

"I wish I could be a writer someday," Elizabeth went on. "Sometimes I write poems and stories. But they probably aren't any good," she added shyly.

Her friend kneeled on the floor and put her elbows on the bed. She stared into Elizabeth's eyes. "I bet they're really, really, really good," she said.

Elizabeth grinned and shook her head. "I don't know."

"I know!" Amy gasped. "You should show

one of your stories to Angela Daley when she comes!"

Elizabeth felt her cheeks get hot. "No," she said, shaking her head from side to side while she spoke. "She wouldn't want to read something a second-grader wrote."

"I bet she would," Amy said, nodding yes just as hard as Elizabeth was shaking her head no.

"You could show it to Mrs. Becker first," Amy said. "She'll tell you if it's good enough to show to Angela Daley."

Elizabeth frowned while she thought about that. More than anything, she wished Angela Daley would read one of her stories and tell Elizabeth if she liked it. "That's a good idea," she said slowly. "I think I will. And you know what?" she added excitedly. "I already have a story idea."

"What? Tell me," Amy said.

"Nope," Elizabeth giggled. "It's a secret."

"If you don't tell me, I'll tell Todd Wilkins that you think he's cute," Amy warned.

Todd Wilkins was a boy in their class. He and Elizabeth often played tag and softball with other kids in the park. Elizabeth thought Todd was really nice, but she didn't want him to know.

Elizabeth made a monster face at Amy. "If you tell Todd anything, I won't talk to you for a million zillion years."

"All right," Amy said. "But can I read your story?"

Elizabeth thought for a moment. "Only after I show it to Mrs. Becker, OK?"

"Good." Amy began to put all of her stuffed animals on the bed. "Now let's play that game again where all the animals are ship-

wrecked on an island and all they have to eat is crackers and mayonnaise and cherry soda."

Elizabeth giggled. They always made up the story as they went along, and it was getting pretty silly. "OK."

But even while they were playing, Elizabeth was thinking about the new story she would try to write. If it was good enough, maybe she really would show it to Angela Daley.

She hoped it would be good enough.

# CHAPTER 4

# The New Jessica

When Jessica arrived at school the next day, she raced to the classroom. She couldn't wait to put her plan into action. She quickly put her books in her desk, and then ran past Lila and Ellen Riteman.

"Hey, Jessica!" Lila called.

Jessica didn't stop to talk with them. She hurried up to Mrs. Becker's desk and stood with a big smile on her face.

"Good morning, Jessica," the teacher said. "Do you have a question?"

Jessica nodded. "If you want, I could take

attendance for you today," she said in her most polite voice.

"Well, isn't that nice of you," Mrs. Becker replied with a smile. "Thank you." She held out the attendance sheet.

Lila and Ellen were watching Jessica. "What is she up to?" Lila asked.

"Cashman, Egbert, Ferris," Jessica read from the attendance list. She acted very important as she made a check mark beside each name. "I'm taking the roll for Mrs. Becker," she explained.

Lila and Ellen looked at each other.

"My father knows someone who knows Angela Daley," Lila told Ellen loudly. "She lives in Los Angeles and goes to lots of parties with movie stars and rock singers and other famous people."

Jessica pretended she wasn't listening, but

21

she felt angry that Lila was such a show-off. She marched up to Mrs. Becker and handed her the list. "I can erase the blackboard if you want," she said.

"But there isn't anything to erase," Mrs. Becker said with a laugh. The blackboard was clean.

"Then I could bang the erasers together," Jessica said. She took the erasers to the window and clapped them to get the chalk dust out. She started coughing.

"My father says he'll invite her to dinner," Lila said. Her voice carried all the way to the window.

Caroline placed her books on her desk. "Jessica, doing this doesn't mean you'll get picked." She realized what Jessica was doing, and then raised her hand. "Mrs. Becker? I'll erase the blackboard if you want when it needs to be!"

Jessica turned and gave Caroline an angry look. Her plan was to show Mrs. Becker what a good, helpful student she was. Then she was sure to get picked. But if Caroline kept butting in, it would be hard!

When Mrs. Becker finally did pick up an eraser at the end of the spelling lesson, Jessica jumped up from her seat. "I'll do that!" she called out.

"I said I'd do it," Caroline shouted.

Mrs. Becker looked surprised. "Well, how about if Eva does it," she asked. Eva got up and began erasing the new spelling words.

Ken Matthews nudged Jessica. "You're acting just like Caroline," he whispered from behind.

Jessica ignored him because, she decided, good students didn't whisper in class. "Mrs. Becker?" she said. "Can I read first today?"

"All right, Jessica," Mrs. Becker said. It was time for reading to start. "We ended with chapter eight yesterday."

Jessica opened her book, sat up straight, and began to read. She was sure her plan would work. But it meant she had to work extra hard. Then Mrs. Becker would notice her.

"That was very nice," Mrs. Becker said when Jessica finished. "You did an excellent job."

"I love reading, that's why," Jessica explained.

Elizabeth looked at her and raised her eyebrows in a startled expression. Jessica just smiled.

"Maybe you'd like to lead the class discussion of Angela Daley's new book when she comes," Mrs. Becker suggested. She waited for Jessica to answer. "Would you?"

Jessica gulped. That sounded like a lot of work.

"You're not going to get picked to help autograph, Miss Goody-Two-Shoes," Lila whispered. "I know it'll be me, anyway."

"I'll do it if Jessica doesn't want to," Caroline interrupted eagerly.

Jessica gave her a fierce look. Then she smiled at the teacher. "I do want to," she said. When Caroline frowned grumpily, Jessica knew she was winning.

"Fine," Mrs. Becker said. "Now, let's go on."

Jessica was already sorry about her decision. Now she would have to read Angela

Daley's new book, and think of some good questions to ask. But Jessica was sure Elizabeth would help her. Then Mrs. Becker would be impressed.

# CHAPTER 5

# Writing a Story

Elizabeth was upstairs in the bedroom she shared with Jessica, trying to write her story. She finished a sentence, read it over and then crossed it out.

"This is dumb," she said out loud. "No one writes stories that sound like this."

Elizabeth knew that she wanted to write about being twins. But so far, her story sounded like a social studies report.

Frowning, Elizabeth tried to balance her pencil on the tip of her finger and thought for a moment.

Angela Daley wrote stories about animals having adventures. That was the kind of story Elizabeth wanted to write, too.

"I know!" Elizabeth said with a happy smile.

She began writing busily. A few times she had to stop and cross something out. But soon her story was three pages long. When it was finished, she began to copy it over onto clean paper.

The more she thought about it, the more Elizabeth liked what she had written. She still felt shy about showing it to her favorite author. But she knew she could trust Mrs. Becker to give her an honest opinion. That way, if it wasn't good enough, Elizabeth wouldn't give it to Angela Daley. But she was keeping her fingers crossed that Mrs. Becker would like it.

"Hi, Liz," Jessica said, startling Elizabeth. Jessica flopped onto her bed and made the stuffed animals bounce onto the floor. "Do you want to play dress up?"

Elizabeth shook her head. She was still recopying her story. "Not right now."

"What are you writing?" Jessica asked curiously.

Elizabeth covered the story with her hands. She felt shy about showing it just yet. "Oh, nothing special," she said. "Just a dumb old story."

"What's it for?" Jessica wanted to know. She lay on her back and pretended she was riding a bicycle in the air.

Elizabeth didn't want her twin to know it was for Angela Daley. That would make her sound like a show-off. "Nothing," she said. "Come on. Let's go play."

Before she stood up, Elizabeth threw the messy first copy of the story into the trash basket and put the neatly written copy in her desk drawer. She decided to wait a couple of days before she showed it to anybody, just to be sure she still liked it.

After dinner, Jessica tried to do her math homework while Elizabeth was taking a bath. It was so boring! And none of the problems were coming out right. She crumpled her piece of notebook paper and aimed for the trash basket. The ball of paper bounced off the rim. She went to pick it up for another try.

When she leaned over, she could see that the trash basket had several crumpled papers in it. Jessica pulled out one sheet and read the first paragraph. It was about two otter sisters who were swimming in the ocean together.

"Otters! My favorites!" Jessica exclaimed. She read some more of the story. She thought it was good.

She couldn't understand why Elizabeth would throw it away. Maybe Elizabeth didn't like it, but Jessica did. She wished she had made it up.

Then Jessica had a great idea. Didn't Elizabeth say she was writing "nothing special"? Since Elizabeth didn't want it, maybe Jessica could copy it over and give it to Mrs. Becker. That would be a great present for Angela Daley!

The more Jessica thought about it, the more she liked her idea. Elizabeth wouldn't mind. After all, she had thrown the story away. But Jessica wondered if that would be cheating.

Then she shook her head. Elizabeth wasn't going to use it. And besides, they were twins—they were practically the same person! So it didn't matter, Jessica decided.

With a happy smile, Jessica sat down and started copying the story over. Once Mrs. Becker read it, Jessica was sure she would be picked!

# CHAPTER 6

## Books! Books! Books!

As soon as Jessica and Elizabeth got to class the next morning, Jessica headed for Mrs. Becker's desk.

"I have to ask her something," Jessica explained to her sister. She didn't want Elizabeth to come with her.

Elizabeth stayed behind. "I'm going to talk to Amy."

Jessica hugged her story tight against her chest and stopped in front of Mrs. Becker's desk. Winston Egbert was there, too. He was showing Mrs. Becker a bookcase made out of shoe boxes he had glued together.

"It falls down a lot, though," Winston said just as the bookcase toppled over. He straightened it and smiled at the teacher. "But it's pretty good, isn't it?"

"Very nice, Winston," Mrs. Becker said. "I'm sure Angela Daley will be impressed."

Jessica thought Winston's bookcase was dumb. Her story was much better. She couldn't wait to give it to Mrs. Becker, and she wished Winston would hurry up.

Finally, it was her turn. "Now, what can I do for you, Jessica?" Mrs. Becker asked.

Jessica held out the papers. "I wrote a story for Angela Daley," she said proudly.

"*You* did?" Mrs. Becker said. "I didn't know you liked to write, too."

"I do," Jessica said, nodding enthusiastically. "I like to read and write a *lot*."

Mrs. Becker looked very pleased. "That's wonderful, Jessica. You're certainly doing a good job in all your classes these days. What's your story about?"

"Otters," Jessica said. "They're my favorite animal."

The teacher smiled. "I remember you telling us that once in science class." She took the story and flipped through the pages. "It sounds like something Angela Daley would write about."

"But *I* wrote it," Jessica said. She gulped and crossed her fingers behind her back. She felt bad about lying, but she couldn't tell Mrs. Becker she wanted the story back.

"I believe you, Jessica." Mrs. Becker put

the story aside to look at later. "Well, I'm looking forward to reading it. But, you know," she added with a smile. "If you keep helping in class, reading aloud, and writing stories, it's going to get harder and harder to tell you two Wakefield girls apart!"

Jessica smiled. But inside, she felt a little bit sad that everyone thought Elizabeth was so much smarter than *she* was.

*I am a good student,* Jessica told herself stubbornly. She decided to prove it even more.

When the class went to the school library during reading, Jessica picked out as many books as she could carry. She marched up to the librarian and put them on the counter with a loud *THUMP!*

"My goodness!" Mrs. Weatherby, the librarian, said. "Are you sure you want to take out all those books at the same time?"

Jessica nodded. "Positive."

Lila and Ellen walked up behind her. They each had one book apiece. Lila's eyes widened when she saw Jessica's stack of books.

"You're reading all of those at once?" she asked. Then she read some of the titles out loud. *"Insects of the World, The Life of George Washington, Spooky Stories and Terrifying Tales.* They're all so different from one another."

Jessica shrugged. "So? I like to read lots of different kinds of books."

Lila and Ellen looked at each other and then giggled behind their hands.

Jessica stuck her tongue out at them. "Just because I like to read doesn't mean you

have to make fun of me," she said. "I'm going to get picked to help Angela Daley because I've read every single one of her books. Elizabeth has them all at home."

She didn't look at her friends when she said that, though, because what she said wasn't true. She had read only the back covers of all of Angela Daley's books. The books were so long that she couldn't read them all and still have time to play.

"So what," Lila said. She stuck her nose in the air. "I don't even have to read the books because my father can introduce me *personally*. And then Mrs. Becker will pick me."

Jessica felt like hitting Lila, but she didn't. Lila and Ellen walked away.

"Did you really read all the books?" Elizabeth asked. She had come up to Jessica very quietly.

Jessica blinked. "Well . . ."

"If you're going to do the class question-and-answer period, you should read them," Elizabeth told her seriously. "I'll help you, if you want."

All of a sudden, Jessica wished she hadn't taken Elizabeth's story. Even if Elizabeth didn't want it, it wasn't Jessica's to take. But Mrs. Becker already had it. It was too late now.

Jessica didn't know what to do.

# CHAPTER 7

# A Sleepless Night

A few nights later, Elizabeth was wriggling around under her covers. She thumped her pillow and tucked her koala bear under her arm. Then she closed her eyes and tried to fall asleep.

Nothing happened.

Sighing, Elizabeth rolled over again and curled up in a ball.

"Are you awake?" Jessica whispered in the darkness.

"Yes," Elizabeth admitted. "I can't fall asleep. I'm too excited."

"Because Angela Daley is coming tomorrow?" Jessica asked.

Elizabeth gulped. "Yes. And also because . . ."

"Because what?" Jessica whispered.

Elizabeth stared at the ceiling. She could see the shadows of tree branches. "Well, I decided to give Angela Daley one of my stories to read."

"One of your stories?" Jessica repeated.

"A new one," Elizabeth said. "I wrote it this week."

There was silence. Elizabeth turned so she was facing the other bed. "Jessie?" she whispered.

"I didn't know you were going to give her a story," Jessica said quietly. "You didn't tell me about it."

Elizabeth felt bad for keeping a secret

from her twin. "I know. I'm sorry I didn't tell you. I didn't even make up my mind until today. Now I'm positive I want to show the story to her. I gave it to Mrs. Becker after lunch. I wanted her to read it first."

"Mrs. Becker?" Jessica squeaked.

"Yes." Elizabeth wondered why Jessica sounded so worried. "I wanted to make sure it's good enough to give to Angela Daley."

There was another long silence. Finally Jessica said, "What's it about?"

Elizabeth giggled. "I'm not telling. It's a surprise. But if Angela Daley likes it, I'll definitely let you read it, OK?"

"You should have turned in one of your old stories," Jessica suggested. She sounded very serious. "I think the story you wrote last year about our trip to Grandma and Grandpa's was really really good."

Elizabeth frowned and hugged her koala bear. She could just see the shape of Jessica's bed in the darkness. She was a little bit puzzled at the way Jessica was acting.

"I think my new one is the best I ever wrote," she said.

Jessica didn't say anything. Elizabeth was pretty sure her sister was upset about something. Twins could always tell things like that.

"Jessie?" she said softly.

"What?"

"Is something wrong?" Elizabeth asked.

Jessica rustled under the covers. "Nothing—it's just that I hope I get picked and I don't know if I will be. Especially if you handed in a story."

"I'm not doing it to get picked!" Elizabeth

explained. "I just want her to read my story."

"Then why don't you get it back from Mrs. Becker and hand it in the day after tomorrow?" Jessica asked nervously.

Elizabeth sat up in bed. "But Angela Daley's coming *tomorrow*. I won't get picked, honest. I bet you will."

"Oh . . ." Jessica sighed. "Well, I'm still nervous about doing the question-and-answer period."

Elizabeth decided that was what her sister was most worried about. "I'll help you, if you want," she offered. "We can think up some good questions on the bus."

She held her hand out and tapped Jessica's bed. Jessica reached out for her sister's fingers.

"I know we're going to have a really good time tomorrow," Elizabeth said.

"I sure hope so," Jessica answered. She sounded far away.

Elizabeth let go of Jessica's hand and curled up under the covers again. The faster she fell asleep, the faster it would be tomorrow!

# CHAPTER 8

# Telling the Truth

Jessica felt terrible when she woke up. What if Elizabeth had handed in the story about the otters? Jessica realized she had made a big mistake. Using Elizabeth's story was a terrible thing to do. She could get into big trouble, and Elizabeth was going to be very angry at her if she found out.

"Good morning, girls," Mrs. Wakefield said when they sat down at the breakfast table.

"Good morning, Mom," Elizabeth said cheerfully.

Jessica gulped her orange juice. She had to think of a way out of the mess she had made. Maybe it wasn't too late. Maybe Mrs. Becker hadn't read the story yet. Somehow, she had to get the story back.

"How am I going to do that?" she muttered.

"What?" Elizabeth asked.

Jessica felt her cheeks warm up. "Nothing," she said.

On the way to school, Jessica tried to think of ways to get the story away from Mrs. Becker. Jessica knew one thing: It was going to be tricky!

When Jessica walked into the classroom, Mrs. Becker was writing spelling words on the blackboard. Jessica walked quietly to the teacher's desk and glanced at the stack of papers.

The story she had handed in was on top!

Jessica tried to swallow the big lump in her throat. Keeping her eyes on Mrs. Becker, she reached her hand out to take the paper.

Mrs. Becker turned around. "Good morning, Jessica," she said, just as Jessica snatched her hand back.

"Hi, Mrs. Becker," Jessica said nervously. Her paper was still sitting on top of the pile.

"Do you have a question?" Mrs. Becker asked.

Jessica didn't know what to say. "Well, um . . ." She saw Lois Waller tying her shoe laces. "I think Lois needs help."

"Lois?" Mrs. Becker called. "Are you OK?"

Jessica reached her hand out again while Mrs. Becker was looking at Lois.

"No, I can do it!" Lois called.

Then the teacher turned around again and saw Jessica pick up the paper.

"Jessica?" Mrs. Becker said. She was frowning now. "Do you need something?"

Jessica's face was bright pink. She blinked quickly. "I, um . . . I wanted to make a correction on my story," she whispered.

Mrs. Becker looked Jessica right in the eye. "I have already read it, Jessica. It's very good." She paused and looked down at the stack of papers. "So is Elizabeth's."

Jessica thought she would cry. "Mrs. Becker?" she asked. "Could I—could you—"

"Yes?" Mrs. Becker said, waiting for Jessica to go on. "Yes, Jessica?"

"I, um . . ." Jessica looked back to where her sister was sitting. Elizabeth saw her and waved. Jessica gulped.

"I don't want you to count that story," Jessica said. She sniffed loudly and twisted one of her shirt buttons around and around. "I didn't—I didn't—"

Mrs. Becker gave Jessica a smile that said she understood. "I know, Jessica. I was very upset by it, but I hoped you would come and tell me the truth. I'm glad you did."

She picked up the story and handed it to Jessica. "You won't do anything like that again, will you?"

"No! I promise!" Jessica said quickly. She gave her teacher a hopeful look. "You won't tell my sister, will you?"

Mrs. Becker shook her head. "No, I won't. But it might be a good idea for you to tell her."

"Me?" Jessica squeaked. She looked over her shoulder at her twin. "I don't want her to know!" she whispered. "Never in a million billion zillion years!"

"Well, it's up to you," Mrs. Becker said. She nodded. "Now, why don't you go sit down, Jessica. Angela Daley will be here any minute now."

Jessica let out a sigh of relief. "OK, Mrs. Becker. Thanks."

Now Elizabeth would never have to find out, Jessica thought happily. She skipped back to her seat with the story in her hand. But just as she reached her desk, she tripped and dropped the papers!

"I'll get them," Elizabeth said, bending down.

"*No!*" Jessica cried. But it was too late.

# CHAPTER 9

# Angela Daley
# Comes to Class

Elizabeth saw the title on the paper she was holding. It said, *The Otter's Daughters* by Jessica Wakefield.

"Jessica!" Elizabeth gasped. "This is my story!"

"Just give it back, Liz. Don't read it!" Jessica begged.

But Elizabeth continued to read. She was puzzled, and hurt, and angry. It was her

story, with Jessica's name on it. She didn't know what to feel.

She looked at her sister. Jessica's eyes were filled with tears. "I'm sorry, Lizzie. I thought you threw it away!" Jessica whimpered.

"You copied my story?" Elizabeth said in a quiet voice. She still couldn't believe it. Her eyes filled up with tears, too.

Just then, there was a knock on the door.

"Mrs. Daley is here, class!" Mrs. Becker announced.

Elizabeth felt like she was being pulled in two directions. Part of her wanted to cry, and part of her wanted to jump up and down with excitement.

A tall woman with wavy gray hair and wearing a bright blue dress walked in. She carried a large bag stuffed with papers and books. Wrapped around her shoulders was a red scarf with a colorful design around the edges.

"She doesn't look like a movie star!" Ellen Riteman whispered to Lila. "You were lying."

Lila's face was bright red.

Jessica realized Lila had made up everything she had said about Angela Daley. But now Jessica didn't even care. She was too upset about Elizabeth.

"Class," Mrs. Becker said. "This is Angela Daley."

"Hello, everyone," Mrs. Daley greeted the class. She put down her bag and took out several books.

"Mrs. Daley's going to answer your questions about being a writer, and then I hope she'll read to us from her new book," Mrs. Becker continued.

"That's right," Mrs. Daley said. She rubbed her hands together, and gave everyone a big smile. "Who has the first question?"

Caroline raised her hand quickly. "Mrs. Daley? Do you have any pets?"

Mrs. Daley nodded. "Yes, I have three dogs named Little Minch, Football, and Garbanzo, two cats named Theodora and Pixie, a snake called Mr. Hister and quite a few tropical fish. They don't have individual names, but I call them the Dudes."

Elizabeth giggled. She couldn't help it. Everyone else laughed, too. She was starting to feel better.

"Where do you live?" Todd Wilkins asked.

"Duro Canyon," the author replied. "Where do you live?"

"Sweet Valley," Todd said. He grinned.

Elizabeth looked over at Amy, and Amy looked back with an excited smile. Angela Daley was fun! Amy raised her hand.

"Yes, Amy?" Mrs. Becker said.

"Where do you get your ideas?" Amy asked shyly. Her cheeks were pink. "I love your animal stories."

"Thank you!" Angela Daley scratched her head, and her scarf slipped off her shoulders. "Well, let me think. Sometimes I just watch my animals, and I imagine what they are thinking. Little Minch especially. He's a very smart dog, and I usually ask his opinion on things."

When everyone looked startled, Angela

Daley grinned mischievously. "Actually, I get ideas from my children, or from remembering what I did when I was growing up. Things like that."

Elizabeth finally had the courage to ask a question. "Are you going to write another book soon?" She held her breath and waited for the answer.

"Yes," the author replied. "There's one I'm working on now. And I'll even read a little bit from it. But first . . ." She trailed off and arched her eyebrows. Everyone waited for her to go on.

"First," Angela Daley said, looking at Mrs. Becker, "I'm going to read a story your teacher gave me. I think it's particularly good."

Elizabeth sat up straight. Angela Daley took a pair of glasses out of her bag and put them on. Then she took out some papers and cleared her throat.

"This story is called *The Otter's Daughters*," she announced.

Elizabeth clapped both hands over her mouth in surprise. Angela Daley was reading her story!

# CHAPTER 10

## Elizabeth's Big Day

Elizabeth's story was about otter sisters who were best friends. While Mrs. Daley read the story, Jessica felt like crying. Jessica was even sorrier she had copied it from her twin because it reminded her that she had the best sister in the whole world.

"'And so the otter twins learned that they could not stay mad at each other for long,'" Mrs. Daley read. She continued. "'The otters walked hand in hand down the forest path until they reached their cozy wooden house. The End,'" Mrs. Daley said. There was silence in the room. "And this story was written by Elizabeth Wakefield."

Jessica felt so proud of Elizabeth she nearly jumped out of her chair. Elizabeth was smiling from ear to ear, and everyone was looking at her. They were all very impressed that she had written such a good story.

"Are you still mad at me?" Jessica whispered to Elizabeth. "I thought you were throwing it away. That's the only reason I took it. I didn't know you still wanted it."

Elizabeth looked down at her desk. "Well . . ."

"Please say you aren't mad, Lizzie," Jessica whispered hopefully. "I told Mrs. Becker the truth and got it back from her. I'll never do it again." She crossed her heart and snapped her fingers twice, which was their secret promise signal.

Elizabeth finally looked at her sister. Then she smiled. "Oh, OK," she mumbled. "I forgive you."

"Phew!" Jessica slumped in her chair. "Thanks," she said.

"Now it's time for the class discussion," Mrs. Becker said. "Jessica?"

"Oops!" Jessica said, jumping up. "I almost forgot!" She looked through all her homework assignments to find the question sheet, then walked to the front of the room. She turned and faced everyone in the class. It was fun to be the center of attention. She looked right at Elizabeth. More than anything, Jessica was glad they were still best friends.

The class discussion lasted ten minutes. Everyone chimed in with answers and suggestions, and Jessica tried very hard to be fair in calling on people. She could tell Mrs. Daley thought she was doing a good job.

No matter how good Jessica was, though, she knew she would never be picked now to help autograph books. She had ruined her chances by handing in a story she had not written. But that was OK, she decided. She thought Elizabeth deserved to win.

"Now, many of you have done something special for our guest," Mrs. Becker said when Jessica went back to her seat. "Lila brought in a beautiful cake that says 'Welcome Mrs. Daley' on it. Caroline brought in a nice glow-in-the-dark pen for signing autographs. Winston made a bookcase, and there are lots of other projects."

"They're all wonderful, too," Mrs. Daley broke in cheerfully. "I'll never be able to decide which is the nicest."

Caroline shot her hand up. "But who gets to help you sign autographs?" she called out.

"Pick Elizabeth," Todd spoke up suddenly.

"Yes!" Ellen agreed. "Pick Elizabeth! She wrote such a good story!"

"Right," Amy said. Everyone else nodded and whispered, "Elizabeth should get picked."

Jessica turned to her sister. Elizabeth looked embarrassed, but she looked happy, too.

"I think it's unanimous, Elizabeth," Mrs. Becker said with a laugh.

Mrs. Daley held out her hand. "Come on up here, Elizabeth. We writers have to stick together."

While everyone watched, Elizabeth slipped out of her seat and walked up to the front of the classroom. Jessica was just as happy as if she had been picked herself. Her very own sister was the star of the day.

"Now," Angela Daley told Elizabeth. "Your job is to hand me the books in my bag while the students come up here. Think you can handle that?"

Elizabeth nodded and gave her favorite author a big smile. "Yes!"

"OK, then," Mrs. Becker said. "Everyone line up!"

Jessica jumped out of her chair. She may not have been picked, but she was going to be first in line!

At the end of the day, Mrs. Becker handed out small slips of paper to everyone in the class.

"What's this for?" Charlie Cashman said loudly.

Mrs. Becker returned to her desk. "These are permission slips. First of all, fill in your name," she said, giving the class a mysterious smile. "Then, where it says 'permission to go to the *blank*', fill in the word zoo."

"The zoo!" Jessica gasped, turning to Elizabeth.

Elizabeth's eyes widened. "The zoo? We're going to the zoo? Really and truly?"

"That's right," Mrs. Becker laughed. "It's the second-grade's annual science field trip. Last year my class went to the Natural History Museum. And this year it's the zoo. Any questions?"

Jessica shot her hand up. "When are we going?"

"Next week," Mrs. Becker said.

"Yippee!" Jessica yelled. "I can't wait to see the monkeys."

"And the snakes," Charlie said. "They're the best."

"Yuck!" Jessica said, making a face. "Let's save the snakes for last. Maybe then we won't have time to see them."

"We'll have time for *all* the exhibits, Jessica," Mrs. Becker said.

Charlie turned around and stuck his tongue out at Jessica.

Jessica crossed her arms in front of her and frowned. She was used to getting her own way!

*What mischief will Jessica get into at the zoo? Find out in Sweet Valley Kids Book #8,* JESSICA'S ZOO ADVEN-TURE.

# SWEET VALLEY KIDS

Jessica and Elizabeth have had lots of adventures in *Sweet Valley High* and *Sweet Valley Twins*...now read about the twins at age seven! You'll love all the fun that comes with being seven—birthday parties, playing dress-up, class projects, putting on puppet shows and plays, losing a tooth, setting up lemonade stands, caring for animals and much more! It's all part of SWEET VALLEY KIDS. Read them all!

| | | | |
|---|---|---|---|
| ☐ | SURPRISE! SURPRISE! #1 | 15758-2 | $2.75/$3.25 |
| ☐ | RUNAWAY HAMSTER #2 | 15759-0 | $2.75/$3.25 |
| ☐ | THE TWINS' MYSTERY TEACHER # 3 | 15760-4 | $2.75/$3.25 |
| ☐ | ELIZABETH'S VALENTINE # 4 | 15761-2 | $2.75/$3.25 |
| ☐ | JESSICA'S CAT TRICK # 5 | 15768-X | $2.75/$3.25 |
| ☐ | LILA'S SECRET # 6 | 15773-6 | $2.75/$3.25 |
| ☐ | JESSICA'S BIG MISTAKE # 7 | 15799-X | $2.75/$3.25 |
| ☐ | JESSICA'S ZOO ADVENTURE # 8 | 15802-3 | $2.75/$3.25 |
| ☐ | ELIZABETH'S SUPER-SELLING LEMONADE #9 | 15807-4 | $2.75/$3.25 |
| ☐ | THE TWINS AND THE WILD WEST #10 | 15811-2 | $2.75/$3.25 |
| ☐ | CRYBABY LOIS #11 | 15818-X | $2.75/$3.25 |
| ☐ | SWEET VALLEY TRICK OR TREAT #12 | 15825-2 | $2.75/$3.25 |
| ☐ | STARRING WINSTON EGBERT #13 | 15836-8 | $2.75/$3.25 |
| ☐ | JESSICA THE BABY-SITTER #14 | 15838-4 | $2.75/$3.25 |
| ☐ | FEARLESS ELIZABETH #15 | 15844-9 | $2.75/$3.25 |
| ☐ | JESSICA THE TV STAR #16 | 15850-3 | $2.75/$3.25 |
| ☐ | THE CASE OF THE SECRET SANTA (SVK Super Snooper #1) | 15860-0 | $2.95/$3.50 |

# SWEET VALLEY TWINS

Buy them at your local bookstore or use this handy page for ordering:

Bantam Books, Dept. SVT3, 414 East Golf Road, Des Plaines, IL 60016

Please send me the items I have checked above. I am enclosing $_____
(please add $2.50 to cover postage and handling). Send check or money
order, no cash or C.O.D.s please.

Mr/Ms _____

Address _____

City/State _____ Zip _____

SVT3-7/91

Please allow four to six weeks for delivery.
Prices and availability subject to change without notice.